WHA
STORE FOR
DANNY?

To Cathy,

Hope you enjoy it

Roger

ROGER
HASTINGS

In memory of
Chris Devonald (The Beast)

GETTING THERE.

The drink-fuelled stags were drawn to the beat of the music, like eager lemmings on their way to a cliff and they staggered as they passed through the streets lined with Bath stone office buildings that had appeared warm and inviting during the day. But now the workers had gone for the weekend, it was dark and the only light warming the area seemed to ooze from the red neon sign advertising 'Rambo's Nightclub.'

When the stags arrived outside the club, they jockeyed for position in a disorderly queue and they began to laugh and joke with each other, speculating on what was going to happen to the Groom, Phil Jones. For this was going to be his last drinking session as a single man and several of his married friends couldn't wait. At last they would have their revenge, as he'd been responsible for many of the drink- related forfeits that they'd been made to suffer on their stag nights.

And after a short wait, they began to shunt their way forward, watched by the beefy, no-necked doormen who marshalled the club's doors. The young men in the party were all relieved when they were having the back of their hands stamped, as this signalled that they'd passed their severe scrutiny. They travelled deeper into the club afterwards and filtered in through the crowded rooms, until they'd homed-in on the Best Man, Pete Smith. Pete was holding onto the kitty money and he'd used some of it to order a large round of drinks, so they could carry on seamlessly, with their debauched night of boozing.

THE STAGS.

The Best Man and the Groom had met whilst studying on the same degree course at University, and in their second year they'd rented a house together with two other students. They'd grown close, especially after Phil's father had died and Pete had unselfishly stayed up talking with Phil into early hours of the morning when he'd sensed that he needed consoling.

Phil had always felt he was a good friend for helping him get through this sad time. The other lads in the house were a good laugh, but they hadn't wanted to share Phil's or anybody else's grief, they'd been too busy getting drunk and enjoying themselves away from their parent's watchful eyes.

In their fourth year, they'd collected their degrees together, dressed in flowing gowns and mortar boards. It was on a hot summer's afternoon in July and their proud families had shared their Graduation Day success, drinking 'Asti' and gorging on strawberries under white marquees, skewered to campus lawns.

Phil hadn't seen much of Pete afterewards as he'd got a job in his uncle's engineering company near Scunthorpe and Phil had stayed working in Bristol. Consequently, Pete hadn't got to know his new friends, so Phil had asked another mate, Steve Harris to organise the night's entertainments.

He'd chosen Steve because he knew he would be able to control the others whilst they were under the influence. But then he had wondered who would control Steve?

Most of the men in the party played football for the 'Totterdown Hotspurs,' where Steve was their star player, as he'd been their top goal scorer every season since he'd joined the club. Phil was their goalkeeper, his large frame had filled the goalmouth and his strong hands had stopped countless balls to keep the 'Spurs' in their usual position at the top of the league, for yet another year.

Phil's friends had been surprised, when he hadn't chosen Steve to be his Best Man, as they could often be seen laughing together in the bar after the games. Steve made him laugh, usually by insulting him for being Welsh. Phil seemed to enjoy his racial haranguing and the ruder he was, the funnier he seemed to find him. He would respond to Steve's ribbing, by rubbishing him or the English at any chance he could get and when he couldn't think of a parry to his rude remarks, he would curse him in Welsh and that was always guaranteed to earn him abuse.

Steve had a mean streak in him and this could be seen regularly when he was playing football. He'd often antagonise the opposition with his vicious tongue and his cynical fouls. It wasn't personal though, he'd do the same to his own team mates when they were playing against him in their training games - he just couldn't help himself. The older members of the team had learnt to ignore his snide remarks by now and would simply curse him and then carry on playing. But, should anybody retaliate, then his response was always the same. 'It's a man's game mate; if you can't take it; then go and play netball.'

And when asked why he did it, he would simply say 'Well, its all part of the game, isn't it?'

Pete, in his official capacity as the Best Man, had felt he had to make the most of Phil's last stag night, particularly as the 'Spurs' had gone out drinking together so regularly in the past. So, he'd invited some of Phil's old pals from Carmarthen to join the party and they'd travelled over the new Bridge in the afternoon and had started their boozing early, greedily knocking back their pints, as if beer was running out in Wales. They were well lubricated by the time they joined the boys from the 'Spurs,' and all of them agreed afterwards, it had been like they'd been partying together for years.

PARTY TIME!

The 'Spurs' had frequented Rambo's Nightclub regularly over the months, ever since the owners had relaxed their rule banning single-sex parties entering the club, and their original fear that trouble would follow had not been warranted as it was renowned for its no-nonsense bouncers.

Rambo's was packed on the stag night and this was due mainly, to a large party of noisy hens who'd made the atmosphere in there, electric. You hadn't needed to be Stephen Hawking to work out who was with them because they were all wearing short, pink mini skirts and cowboy hats trimmed with tinsel. The hens had arrived early and had secured their seats around the dance floor, which they had done German-style, but not with their towels - they'd used their drinks, jackets and handbags to reserve their places.

The resident, loud-mouthed DJ, M.C. Sparks had done a fine job schmoozing the hens onto the dance floor and they'd danced there in a happy shrieking brood, corralled together by the low brick wall that was surrounding the floor. It was lit from above with ultra violet lights that flashed on and off in tune with the music and they'd made their clothes appear fluorescent and their teeth shine whiter than white, as if they were in a cheesy, American, TV commercial.

HI-JINX IN THE CLUB.

Steve Harris enjoyed the drinking games he played when he was out with the boys and he'd earned his nickname because of them. He was now known as 'Judge Harris' or simply 'The Judge' because he'd always officiated in the Kangaroo Court's that were held on their drinking sessions. He'd filled the position so often, he carried a wig and a little black cloth with him, which he'd wear, when he was sentencing somebody for one of the bogus crimes he'd invented - once he'd found them guilty, of course.

The Best Man and the Groom could not to escape the wrath of 'The Judge' on this last stag night and as soon as they had their drinks in their hands they were whisked off by the men into a quiet corner of the club. The party members crowded around them and made a makeshift courtroom. This had screened the proceedings from the rest of the people in the club and they were charged here by 'The Judge,' with being Welsh gays. It didn't seem to matter, that neither of them was gay and that Pete wasn't even Welsh! A point he'd informed the jury of several times, by shouting out 'I'm not Welsh you morons, I'm from bloody Scunthorpe!'

But, his protests were ignored by the jury, who were determined to see both of them punished and with 'The Judge' residing the verdict would only ever go one way. Phil had been on enough of these occasions, to realise that there was little or no hope of escaping punishment. But, to give them their best chance, he'd chosen Adam McClelland to defend them. This was because: a). Adam was a law student, so he figured he would know the law and b). Because he was Scottish, he thought he'd make a stronger case on behalf of his Celtic cousins and to be fair, he did try.

On his first attempt, he tried to shift the blame from them onto their parents, arguing that 'It was their parents, who brought them into the world as Welshmen, so they were the ones who should be punished.'

But, 'The Judge' was quick to destroy this line of defence, by adding 'Their parents are not in court to answer charges made against the defendants and anyway, the Best Man doesn't seem to know where he comes from.'

The men howled and hooted at this, showing their approval with rowdy cheers and then 'The Judge' began to lecture Adam.

'If you're seriously thinking about entering the legal profession young man, then the first thing you should learn, is who your defendants are. Please note; I would like this woeful attempt at a defence to be wiped from the court's records.'

He'd said this as if a court stenographer was recording his every word and he'd hoped it would undermine Adam's confidence, but Adam appeared to be unruffled by 'The Judge's' rude comments and continued with the charade after the noise had died down.

'The defendants can prove they are not gay your honour and they have assured me that they can bring several female witnesses into court to testify to the fact.'

The crowd murmured their disapproval at this because they hadn't liked Adam's clever new line of defence and they began to boo him for it. But, there was no fear of him persuading the jury that they were innocent and 'The Judge' replied.

'You can't expect the court to wait for evidence of the defendant's sexual conquests, especially, as I am certain none would materialise anyway, and even if they could find some girls silly enough to perjure themselves in front of the court, no one would believe they'd done it willingly and then the defendants will end up facing rape charges as well.'

The jury laughed and cheered his response, as he'd crushed Adam's defence again. So, Adam tried flattery next:

'I must appeal to your honour's good sense of justice, it's not the defendant's fault that they are attractive to both sexes, it's because they have been blessed with rugged good looks; not unlike your honour.'

'Says who?' A voice from the back of the crowd shouted out and the cheers and jeers erupted again, followed by chants of 'Hang the Welsh gays.'

'The Judge' tried to calm them and he called for order in a crescendo:

'Order!......Order!......Order in the court!

 And eventually, he was able to quell their noise, and continue.

 'I must say, that I find this case very disturbing and by listening to the Defence Councillor's accent, it appears that he too is Welsh. And by his own admission, he's not only taken a fancy to the defendants, but even worse, it sounds like he's taken a fancy to me!'

 He pulled a long face, showing he was appalled by prospect of this and the noise from their cheering hit a new peak in response to his play acting.

 Adam wasn't pleased, he didn't like his accent being confused with Welsh because he was a proud Scot, but he'd realised that Steve was trying to intimidate him and so he hadn't retaliated. He'd also understood now, that he was wasting his time in trying to clear Phil and Pete of the charges and if he wasn't careful, he too might suffer at the hands of the English Judge and his jury. So, he didn't waste any more time, he advised the defendant's to change their plea.

 'It seems my clients don't have a case to offer the court your honour, and therefore I must strongly advise them to change their plea to...........

 'GUILTY!'

 This cowardly act of self- preservation had virtually sentenced the 'Welsh lambs to the slaughter.' Phil and

Pete had been disgusted by his treachery and they told him so. However, the jury was pleased by it and several of them patted him on the back whilst chanting-

'GUILTY! GUILTY! GUILTY!'

The men all signalled to 'the Judge' with their thumbs down, as if they were Romans condemning gladiators to death in the amphitheatre and 'The Judge' slowly fished out a pair of round spectacles from a shirt pocket and placed them on the end of his nose. He'd done this because he believed they made him look more learned when he gave his verdict, which he began in his best Judge's voice-

'Having carefully considered the evidence put before me by the Defence council, I find myself with no option but to find the defendants…………....................……….Guilty! As charged.'

Their cheers hit a new volume level and he placed the black sentencing cloth on top of his wig to advise the jury and the prisoner's of their impending fate.

'The defendants have been found guilty in my opinion, of a most heinous crime and therefore, it's only fitting that the punishment I pronounce be one that reflects the seriousness of it. But, I must say, I take no pleasure when sentencing them both to …………….........a De-Welshing!'

The cheers that followed were deafening and 'The Judge' had to wait for the noise to die down before he could finish off the sentence.

'………as I feel, we must purge the Welshness from them.'

The resulting cheers were the loudest yet and they seemed to go on forever. Steve had a wicked smile on his face now, he'd been pleased by the response to his night's, evil, legal work.

THE PUNISHMENT.

The jury closed in around Phil and Pete and stripped them of all their clothing except their socks and they'd only left those on because they thought it made them look silly. They'd realised that resistance was futile and so they hadn't bothered.

Steve handed the lynch mob some manacles that he'd had made by a friend and a couple of the jury members chained the prisoner's ankles with them. After the padlocks had snapped shut, the keys were handed back to 'The Judge' for safe keeping and he proceeded to warn the prisoners-

'You are to wear these shackles for the rest of the night and should either of you be seen without them, then further punishment will be administered to you.'

He reached inside two white carrier bags that were patiently waiting between his feet and he produced some foul smelling leeks from them, which he handed to each of the prisoners. He told Pete to 'lash Phil's – 'Hairy Welsh rump with them fifty times.' And then told Phil to do the same to 'Pete's skinny white arse.' The crowd made sure that the punishment was carried out, while Steve collected some more money from them with a whip-round. He went to the bar and used the new found funds, to purchase lethal cocktails for the two unfortunates.

He'd asked the barman to pour half a pint of lager into two pint glasses and then a shot from everything else he could see in the optics. The piéce de resistance was when he added generous measures of Worcester sauce into the mix, which was considered a nice touch by the others. After a good stir, he poured the cocktails into their left shoes and handed them back, explaining what they had to do next by way of an impromptu rhyme.

'Drink the evil brew, down in one will do, and don't let your lips leave the leather or we'll think of something worse for you to do.'

The prisoners took to their unpleasant task with little or no complaint, which was a surprise, as it had churned the stomachs of everybody else who was watching them and the jury had all groaned as if they had been made to drink it.

Phil completed his task remarkably quickly, but then he had spilt most it down his hairy chest and the liquid followed a route circumnavigating his large, round beer belly until finally, it dripped off him into his socks. He ignored the discomfort of it and wiped the remains of the sticky froth from around his mouth with one of his big hairy wrists. He was grinning now, pleased that he'd managed to finish his potion way before Pete, and he unleashed a long, loud, exaggerated belch as if he was a proud elephant seal on a beach, thus proving, he was the dominant male.

Pete was still struggling with his elixir because it had made him gag. This delayed him and it took him several attempts to finish off his drink and the noisy, baying crowd jeered him all the time, revelling in his obvious discomfort until finally, the drink was drunk. Phil's eyes had begun to glaze over now as the alcohol took effect and it was at this point he decided to make a little speech to his friends-

'I'd like to thank you all for the drink and I must say that drinking English beer in this fashion, has totally improved the taste of it. So much so, I think I'll drink it like this more often.'

His friends cheered him and they were still laughing at him, when he and Pete had to make a 'Keystone Cop' style dash to the toilets. Phil had realised, that he needed to get there as soon as possible to avoid the embarrassment of being sick in the club and unfortunately Pete had not been able to keep up with him. The chain anchored to his ankle had tugged Phil's leg backwards making him trip, and he flew through the toilet door head first nearly tearing it from its hinges. His forward momentum was only stopped after he'd head-butted one of the urinals, which nearly knocked him senseless. His face, slid slowly down the cold, wet, yellowing porcelain and he ended up in a crumpled mess on the toilet floor.

Pete had arrived shortly afterwards as he was still tethered to the other end of the chain, and he quickly yanked Phil's head out of the urinal.

He dragged him back up onto his feet and they both made a synchronized dive for the white wash basins, where they vomited violently together in unison.

After throwing several cupped handfuls of cold, refreshing water into their faces, they began to revive a little and they would have probably been alright then if they'd been allowed to stop drinking - but they weren't. As stars of the night, they were forced back into the circle of men forming the court, and as soon as they'd returned, one of Welsh lads shouted out-

'There seems to be rain in the air tonight lads!' The men all realised what that meant, and they began flicking their beer from their glasses onto Phil and Pete, drenching them, whilst singing-

'We're singing in the rain, singing in the rain,
what a glorious feelin, we're happy again.'

The shower, quickly dried up because two of the bouncers who had been watching from the sidelines decided their antics had gone far enough and they'd ordered them to stop. Phil and Pete were told to get dressed and then one of the bouncers said in a mock Welsh accent-

'After all boys; this isn't a Gay bar, now is it?'

And, the cheers erupted again.

ROUNDING UP THE STAGS.
FRIDAY 3.00AM.

Steve had decided it was time to inflict some more pain and embarrassment on poor Phil, who could barely stand by now. He figured it would make it a more memorable night for him, the more he suffered and it would also enforce his own standing amongst the boys, who already thought, he was 'A right evil bastard.'

He began rounding up the stags who'd scattered into the club as the night wore on and although most of them had carried on drinking with Phil, three of them he'd found dancing and two of them were sat next to hens. He'd ordered all of them to return to the stag party or face retribution in his court and he also advised them, that the stags were leaving soon to give Phil his final punishment.

He left them to make their excuses to the girls and then walked into the bar room like a gunslinger entering a Western saloon. He was still looking for the last straying member of the party and his height advantage had allowed him to peer over the heads of the thirsty clubbers who were waiting at the bar. He picked him out immediately, it had been easy because Danny was wearing his favourite multi-coloured shirt; it was the one he always wore on their drinking sessions.

He'd rarely wash it, except with beer and sweat and then an hour or so before going out; he'd hang it outside his window to air. His fiancée, Sharon, hated this shirt and she'd tried to throw it away on several occasions, but he'd always managed to rescue it. His shirt was sacred to him as it unlocked many wonderful memories of past drinking sessions.

Danny was perched on a stool at the end of the long bar, surrounded by impatient punters needing a drink. He'd been so desperate to sleep, he was resting his head on his arms, using them as a pillow. Steve had arranged three stag nights in as many nights and Danny had been on all three of them. The over indulgence of alcohol and the lack of sleep, had begun to have a dramatic effect on him now, but even so, it was unbelievable, the way he could switch off to the noise of music and the people jostling around him at the bar - it was a gift. And, this hadn't been the first time he'd fallen asleep in an unusual place. Sharon had caught him napping at a disco once, using a speaker as his pillow and she'd commented to friends - 'He's so dozy; he could sleep through a bleedin hurricane!' And, on this night, he probably could.

Steve skilfully muscled his way towards Danny with a few, 'scuse me's,' and a couple of the men he disturbed along the way thought he was pushing in and nearly said something rude to him. But when they saw how big he was, they just put their thumbs up and said, 'Okay mate.' Steve ignored them and as soon as he'd arrived at Danny's side, he playfully punched him on the arm. The shock of it, nearly knocked him off his stool.

'Twat!' Danny spat-out nastily, without opening his eyes to see who had woken him in such an annoying fashion. Steve just laughed at his insult, they were good mates and they'd known each other since the early days at Gresham Road Primary School. Danny began adjusting his sitting position and Steve shouted out to him.

'Lager, Dan?

Danny had slumped back down on his arms again, trying to ignore everyone, but on hearing the offer of a drink he slurred 'Cheerz mate!' and he'd forced back a burp.

'Want a shot as well? We'll be going soon,' Steve suggested thoughtfully.

He ignored his kind offer and then he began to wonder, *how come he never gets drunk?*

He quickly changed his mind about the drink as he didn't want the effort of trying to lift a heavy glass again, and he said-

'On second foughts, Stee, I'll pass, thans may. I've jus bout ad it?'

'What?' Steve shouted out because Danny's words were broken, due to the consumption of excessive alcohol and the noise of the music. Frustratingly for Danny, he had to repeat it again, only louder this time and Steve replied with a disbelieving 'What?' But

Danny ignored him and slid over the bar top to be nearer him with his head still resting on his arms. He hadn't had the energy to raise it up again. So he pulled Steve down to his level and began to plead with him-

'Hey mate, tell me, ee's not 'avin 'nother bleedin stag night, I can't take no more. I took the week off work, 'an this, is the third un I've been on, an I don' fink I'll make 'is wedding, if ee as 'nother.'

'It's ok mate, this is it now, he's having a rest from drinking after tonight. He told me he's going to a trial wedding with Wendy and the vicar or something tomorrow.'

'Than Chrise!' Danny shouted and Steve laughed at him and then began to remind him of the Wedding timetable.

'He's getting spliced at two o'clock on Saturday, so there won't be time to fit in another session, although, the gang's meeting up in the Queen's Head at noon, so, I hope we'll see you there?'

Danny sat up to attention, 'courze!' he replied indignantly. He'd been hurt, that Steve had felt the need to ask him.

'Wherezee now?' Danny enquired.

'He was in the bog being sick again the last time I saw him, it must have been something he ate,' Steve quipped and they laughed.

'The boys want to put him on a train to Carmarthen because he he's always banging on about how Welsh he is. So, I think we'll send him 'Home again to Wales.'

he sang in his best Welsh accent, which sounded more like he worked for an Indian call centre and Danny told him so. They laughed again and Steve continued-

'......I don't know if we'll manage it though; 'Smithy's sobered up a bit now and he's playing mum. He was saying something about a promise he made to Wendy that he'd look after him for her and I think he might try to stop it happening. He'll probably be backed by the Welsh boys too because they're staying at Phil's place tonight and they need to get him home or they'll be sleeping rough. Do you know what I heard? Wendy thought I might 'do something wicked to Phil' and I must say I was hurt by that.'

'Yeah, I bet,' Danny replied, grinning at him.

Steve began to smile too; he knew what everybody thought about him.

'Anyway, the talk is, that if Pete kicks up too much fuss, we're going to tape him up to Phil and send them both back to Wales. Let's face it, they are Welsh Gays.'

They laughed again.

'Servz 'im right for spoilin our fun, hey mate,' Danny said joking with him, and then flopped his head back down on his arms again, when he realised how tired he was.

'Mus sleep, mus sleep,' he groaned.

'Come on Danny you big girl, wake up or you'll be going to Wales with them.' Steve shouted in his ear.

Danny jumped up because he realised Steve,

probably wasn't joking and he used his last ounce of energy to slide off his stool. He almost keeled-over because his knees were weak from sitting awkwardly and when he'd tried to stand up straight again, he couldn't because his left leg had gone to sleep. So, he began stamping his foot on the floor in, an attempt to get his circulation going again and some of the people watching his little dance began to laugh at him.

'Mus tav drunk more than I fought,' he said joking.

'Must have,' Steve replied, grinning at him.

'Right, let's get 'Taffy' on th' train an then I got t'get t'sleep, cos Shaz's makin me go shopin in th' morning to get 'is presen, an I bet she'll be early.'

DANNY'S FLAT. FRIDAY 8.45AM.

Danny was woken from his comatose sleep by the sound of his door buzzer, it was buzzing like a demented wasp and he began to curse it in his head, but, it wouldn't stop. So, he rolled off his bed in a grizzly bear mood and stumbled on a trainer he'd discarded the night before. He cursed out loud and then hobbled off in the direction of his front door.

The buzzing sound was grating his nerves and he knew he would have to stop it, so he staggered forward with his eyes wide shut and his arms stretched out like Frankenstein's monster. He was moving more cautiously now, but, he still managed to trip, this time on another trainer that was parked in the middle of his room. He grabbed hold of his toes yelping with the pain and he began hopping around, as if on a pogo stick. Eventually, this eased his pain and soon he became aware of the annoying buzzing sound again.

'Alright! Alright! I'm bloody coming, shut up can't you?' He croaked, his throat was dry after the stag night celebrations and when he finally reached the door, he fumbled around until he found what he was looking for. He twisted the door catch with automatic proficiency and it clicked open.

He stuck his head out into the hallway looking to see who was there and he could barely focus through the watery haze that was blurring his eyes.

All he could see was a blonde-haired fur ball and after straining for a few more seconds his eyes began to clear, it was Sharon his girlfriend, and she was looking pretty good this morning. She was dressed in tight jeans and a low cut tee- shirt that displayed her ample cleavage and more than a glimpse of tummy.

'Halloooo!' She sang out cheerfully which made him wince. The only trouble with her this morning was, that she was too damn cheerful and he didn't feel a bit of cheer, in fact, he didn't even want to speak. All he could manage, was a grumpy -

'Oh it's you.'

'And what's up with Mr. Misery Guts this morning,' she said smiling sweetly at him, although she really didn't need to ask. She must have seen how tired he looked and she should have realised he would have a hangover. He closed his eyes again and he tried to smile at her, which made him look like he was doing a Stan Laurel impersonation and the only thing he needed to do to improve on his impression, was to scratch his head.

Sharon took a pace backwards and studied him for a moment; he was stood before her, dressed only in boxer shorts and one black sock. He needed to shave badly, his eyes were closed and his hair resembled the aftermath of a Tsunami. Danny had only recently turned twenty four, but this morning, he looked and felt like he was ninety.

'Oh my God! You look a right bloody mess Danny

Walker. Is this what I'm going to wake up to when we get married?' She said joking with him.

'Only, if you're bloody lucky. What do you have to be so soddin loud for in the mornin?' he said miserably.

'Well that's bloody charming, that is, what about, a hello darling; it's lovely to see you or something; I haven't seen you all week,' she replied as if she was hurt.

'Well, if you'd been through what I have over the last three days, you wouldn't be so damned cheerful, not at this ungodly hour.'(Score 1- 0), he thought, as if he was playing an imaginary game of football and he'd scored a goal against her.

'It's not that early and it's your own damned fault, you shouldn't have gone out on all three stag nights, you're a greedy drunken pig. (Score 1-1), she'd started playing his game.

'You have to do these things for your friends Sharon, as you know, it's traditional and you only get married once.' (Score 2-1), he snapped at her indignantly and then, he'd tried to give her a peck on the cheek before she could reply. But, she wasn't having it, she pulled away from him and he missed her.

'Ged off me you big ape! You won't get around me like that, you haven't shaved, you're all prickly and you stink of beer.'(Score 2-2)

'Actually, its designer stubble dear and that's my after shave you can smell, it's 'Midnight in the Gas Works, by canal' and he grinned at his old joke.

But, Sharon was not impressed, she tutted and her eyes flicked up to the sky because she'd heard him say it, too many times before.

'..........and you wouldn't be moaning like that if it was Brad Pitt stood before you, now would you?' He continued. (Score 3-2)

'No, you're right there,' she replied dreamily and then she quickly turned on him again,

'But then, you're not Brad Pitt, are you?'(Score 3-3) Danny looked at her, feigning hurt and with doe-like eyes, he said softly,

'No, but Brad Pitt's not marrying you on September 26th is he my cherub.'(Score 4-3)

Sharon didn't fall for his patter, she knew him too well.

'No, more's the pity.'(Score 4-4)

Danny stuck out a furry tongue at her in response; he couldn't be bothered to carry on with the game, (Game over, 4-4, it's a draw).

He allowed the door to open wider and she barged- in past him. She stopped dead, frozen in her tracks when she saw the mess in his living room/bedroom. His clothes were strewn over chairs, X- box games littered the floor, empty cups nurtured moulds and small fruit flies flitted around the Chinese take-away wrappers that were littering his coffee table.

'What a bloody mess. This place looks like a news report from Beirut and it stinks, it smells like a Chinese brewery in here.

Open the bloody window can't you and let some fresh air in.'

Danny ignored her moaning , he just grinned at her and then glanced at the white mark on his wrist where his watch should have been, but there was only wrist.

'What time is it?' he enquired.

Sharon looked at her mobile phone and squawked-

'Good garden peas, its ten past nine already!' Then she sighed and said-

'Come on, hurry up, have shower and don't forget to shave, you look like a bloody tramp. We've got such a lot of shopping to do.'

'Noooooo! He cried out dramatically, as if he was in pain. 'No Shaz, I can't, not shopping, not this morning, can't you see I'm ill?'

'I've no sympathy for you, Danny, it's all self inflicted, so shut up and get a move on. They're your friends as well as mine and you wouldn't go shopping last weekend because of that silly game of football. They're getting married tomorrow, so we have to find a present today. (Score 4-5) I've taken a day off work to go shopping with you, and I'm fed up of finding presents on my own. (Score 4-6) It serves you right, and as you say, it only happens once, so you better start taking some responsibility and I don't suppose you've thought of what we can buy them?'

Danny shook his head.

'No, I didn't think you would, it's always left up to me.'(Score 4-7)

'But, you're so good at it Shaz,' he said, trying to flatter her. (Score 5-7)

'Well that may be, but you're still coming with me. I'm going to the newsagents now, to buy some fags, so you'd better be ready when I get back and don't forget your wallet, cos you're buying me Breakfast.'(Score 5-8)

She was grinning as she left his flat and she was thinking (Score 5-8, now the game's over, and I win).

Danny walked into his bathroom miserably and he felt like he'd lost the FA cup final on penalties. (Score 5-8. Game over).

THE SUNSET TERRACE BAR (NEAR THE SHOPS). FRIDAY 10AM.

Sharon was looking around at the people sitting in the schizophrenic 'Sunset Terrace Bar'. It was usually full of young, drunk people at night, but in the daytime it reverted back into a sober café, full of resting shoppers. Danny had chosen it, so they could sit outside in the fresh air, and although it was September, it wasn't too cold. Sharon drank the last dregs of her coffee, having polished off a full English breakfast in front of him. He hadn't eaten any of his. He'd felt sick at the thought of it.

She began to pick at the food he'd left on his plate although she really wasn't hungry any more, she was bored. Danny was too tired to make the effort of talking to her and he was trying his best to snatch some sleep. She'd exhausted her interrogation of him, grilling him for information about the last three days and nights, but he'd found it hard to recollect anything about the stag celebrations, even the one the night before. Although he had remembered, they hadn't put Phil and Pete on a train to Carmarthen because none of them had bothered to check the train times and by the time they'd arrived at the station, the last train had gone.

Phil and Pete had been relieved, when they'd only been stripped and bound naked to a lamp post outside a police station. The men had decided a sign was necessary, but nobody had brought a pen with them. So Danny painted a primitive message with a stick and some mud on the back of a dismantled estate agent's sign that he'd found in a garden. He'd scribed 'We hate pigs!' and tied it around Phil's neck.

After completing this last chore, he'd realised, that he'd had enough, so he'd switched onto automatic pilot and staggered off into the night. He'd tried to quick march a few times to get home faster, but stopped, after he'd walked into some privet hedges and fell over a garden wall into some rose bushes.

Sharon usually enjoyed 'people watching,' but now she was beginning to tire of it and she tried to get some more conversation out of Danny again-

'I s'pose it's okay to smoke out here,'

Danny didn't answer her and she lit up anyway. An old lady, looked at her in disgust, obviously not impressed by the assault on her atmosphere, but, she wasn't brave enough to say anything to Sharon. The big clue for Sharon should have been the absence of ashtrays on the tables, but she'd improvised, by flicking her ash into her saucer.

Danny had a wicked headache and he felt like death. His eyes had closed again and he would have been asleep if Sharon hadn't been there. He began to total the number of hours he'd slept over the last three nights and he figured it was only nine. Roughly, three per night, and oh! How he wished, he'd stayed in bed during the days to recover from the partying now.

But, he hadn't; he'd gone Paintballing on one day and Karting on another. Steve had organized an impromptu game of football on the Downs on the second evening and there'd been the customary drinking in bars afterwards, and at the time it had been great fun.

Sharon was very bored now and she blew a mouthful of blue smoke into his face to reward him for not talking to her. He began coughing and said-

'Do you have to Shaz, (cough), you know I don't feel too good this morning.'

She grinned at him wickedly, pleased by her little revenge and then she then she began looking around at the families and old people in the cafe again.

'I feel bloody lousy,' he mumbled, trying to make a conversation, although, he wasn't really expecting an answer or sympathy for that matter and he received neither. They'd been going out with each other for too long for that, it was nearly seven years now.

Sharon knew exactly what she was taking on by marrying Danny and she'd told her friends recently-

'He's pretty good these days, he doesn't drink half as much as he used to.'

This was because he usually ended up having to drive them around when they went out together and this suited her because she enjoyed a large glass or two, herself. He would compensate for this, by telling his friends 'I can take it or leave it these days.'

However, this did not apply to football club drinking sessions and definitely not on stag nights.

Sharon enjoyed nagging him and he'd let her get away with it most of the time, only offering the odd sarcastic comment back to her in return and now she'd started on him again-

'I've no sympathy for you Danny; you should have left the party earlier and got some sleep.'(Score 1-0)

Danny wanted to ignore her, especially as he'd heard this nag once already, but he still took the bait.

'And you've never had a drink I suppose?' He knew the answer to his question. It was 'plenty of times.'

Sharon grinned at him; she knew how to wind him up and he continued with his argument.

'….And you can't leave a stag night early, I'm sure I would have got away with that, on my best mate's stag night.'(Score 1-1)

'Since when was Phil your best mate, I thought Steve was? And anyway, it was his third stag night, so of course you could have.'(Score 2-1) She knew this would rattle his cage.

'Yeah, whatever!' he replied grumpily. (Score 2-1) Game over.

'Well, we can't go on chatting here all morning; we've got to get something for them today. Can't you think of anything yet?'

'I thought you looked at the wedding list and said we'd buy towels,' he responded wearily.

'That was just one idea and we might find something better in the Sales.'

She stood up quickly having realised she was wasting her time in discussing it with him. She stubbed her cigarette out, picked up her handbag and a carrier bag containing a blouse she wanted to return.

'Come on; let's try 'Marks's,' and no whining.'

'Oh lets!' He replied sarcastically and luckily she hadn't heard him because he wasn't ready for another ear bashing. He rose to his feet slowly, pushing his chair backwards and it made a 'nails on blackboard' type of screech on the polished floor tiles. He manoeuvred himself around the tripping hazards; the carrier bags, small children, tables and chairs and they returned to the endless stream of shoppers in the high street. They went with the flow until eventually, they'd arrived at 'the shop of dreams,' well; it was in Sharon's mind, the one known to us lesser mortals as 'Marks & Spencer.'

FRIDAY 4.30PM.
STILL SHOPPING.

Sharon led Danny into the shops like a Red Indian brave on the trail of a wounded animal and he plodded along behind her, like a trusty old mule. He hated shopping and was aware that he was only there to carry her bags. He'd always been an impulse buyer and this had enabled him to leave the shops as quickly as possible. When he was out shopping with her, he didn't bother to look for anything anymore because she would always tell him, there was somewhere cheaper to buy it from. Sharon was an expert and he knew no one better at it.

Danny was looking for something, *anything,* that he could sit down on to take the weight off his aching feet. If he could just find a chair or a sofa, he would close his eyes and catch up with some sleep. He began to muse now, in his sleepy, drug-like state *After all the years of training and all the games of football, it has never prepared me for a shopping trip with Sharon.*

She might as well have been shopping by herself and she knew it. Normally she would give in to his whining, saying-

'You might as well go home; you're no bloody help to me, not with your constant moaning.'

But this time, she was determined that he would stay with her as he'd always got out of it in the past and with their wedding day barely a year away now, she was thinking of the wedding gifts that she would like to receive from their friends and relations. And who knows, if Danny was out shopping with her, he might be persuaded to buy something for them.

The couple had been eagerly watching the progress of the builders, who were building their new home and they hoped it would be ready for them, when they returned from their honeymoon. The builders had promised... so maybe it would be?

As she looked around for the wedding present, she'd dropped hints to him, like-

'Oh, look at that Danny, that's nice isn't it? That would look good in our place' and she'd said it a few times already. But, after saying it this time, there'd been no confirmation from him and she'd realised, that Danny wasn't with her. She looked around and spotted him. He'd found a vacant chair by a pillar to sit on and his eyes were closed. A shop assistant was looking at him, resting there so innocently, totally oblivious to his surroundings and teetering on sleep. She looked up at Sharon and she smiled at her, with an understanding, smile. But, Sharon was unforgiving,

'Men, bloody useless aren't they,' she said to her and then she screamed at him-

'Wake up Danny, for God's sake!'

He jumped up and stood to attention as if he'd been caught, sleeping on guard duty by a Sergeant Major.

'Come on, we're going now. You're so bloody embarrassing; we'll try that new Superstore 'Dempsey's' next. Mary Reed told me they've got everything there and her sister Karen has got her wedding list with them. We must sort ours out soon and we can look for things for us, while we're there. We should have gone there first really, do you know, I'd almost forgotten about it.'

Oh yippee! He thought as he followed her out of the store and they rejoined the shoppers in the street again. They dummied around them, like rugby players, until finally, they'd arrived outside the revolving doors in front of Dempsey's.

'Did I tell you? I'm meeting the girls tonight at Wendy's house for the 'Night before Party' and we're going to have an Indian from 'The Raj.' So, we'll have to hurry because Dempsey's closes at six and we won't have long to look.' She'd informed him of this as if it was his fault they were entering into the store and Danny smiled and he was thinking *Yeees! There is a God*. He couldn't wait for this shopping nightmare to end and then he would go home and crawl under his lovely, warm, duck down duvet and get some sleep.

DEMPSEY'S SUPERSTORE.
FRIDAY 5.45PM.

Dempsey's had been converted into a Superstore from two red brick, Victorian warehouses and it was so large, it advertised itself as 'The Biggest and Best in the West!' And it certainly was the biggest. It sold Designer Clothes, Perfumes, Electrical Goods, Furniture, DIY products, Wines and Spirits; in fact there wasn't much you couldn't buy in there.

'Oh look Danny, its massive!' Sharon squealed with delight as they entered the store via the revolving doors made of brushed steel and grey tinted glass. She was excited at what they might find in there, but he was mortified. He'd closed his eyes in horror when he saw it and he began to moan at her again-

'I'm sorry Shaz, I just can't take any more, I'll have to leave you to it, I can't go on shoppin', I'm ill and I've got to get some sleep, please let me go.' He was begging her now, clasping his hands together in mock prayer, like a guilty player to a football referee.

But Sharon was made of sterner stuff and she wouldn't give in to him, not this time.

'Typical, you've no bloody staying power, come on, they shut soon and then you can go home, you big wimp!'

He capitulated again, and very soon they were travelling up the escalator to the fourth floor.

Sharon realised they would have to be quick if she wanted to see the whole store and the best way she figured, was to work her way down through it.

On reaching the top floor, they entered via the Furniture Department and immediately, Sharon saw a cream coloured leather three piece suite that she thought 'was to die for.' But, Danny's eyes had zoomed off in the opposite direction as he'd seen an armchair with a broken leg in front of some broken chairs and other damaged goods. The armchair was partially obscured by a wardrobe, and it was this, that he'd found so appealing. The armchair seemed to say to him, 'Come on Danny, come and sit down on me.'

He needed no more persuading, he took the shortest route to it and then collapsed down on it with a loud, blissful sigh. He'd closed his eyes, only meaning to do it for a short while, but as soon as he had, he'd fallen asleep because he couldn't stay awake a moment longer.

Sharon entered the maze of three piece suites, and her eyes were blinkered to everything else around her. She was speed shopping now and she hadn't got time to think about Danny and what he was up to. She'd just shouted over her shoulder to him from time to time, assuming that he would be there.

'Oh look Danny, look at that suite, oh! I'd love one like that.' She'd said, not waiting for his reply and then sat down on it and entered into a romantic dream. She'd imagined herself curled up on it, dressed in a white, silk gown next to an open fire, sipping hot chocolate and stroking a long haired, white cat. She'd stayed in her ecstasy for less than a minute, before shooting back up onto her feet like an Exocet missile and she moved quickly on to the next suite and the next dream, she was in shopping heaven. It had been a total mystery to Danny why she was looking in the Furniture Department, when they had such an urgent present to buy, but, that was Sharon for you.

Sharon had already left the Furniture Department, before she'd realised that he wasn't with her any more. She'd called him on his mobile phone, but she hadn't been able contact him and she hadn't got time to go looking for him.

So, she carried on without him, and finally found the wedding present for the happy couple on the second floor, thus saving her shopping reputation. She'd bought a bale of dark blue towels, which had been her original idea and she'd been pleased with them because she'd managed to buy them a lot cheaper than she'd expected. On leaving the Linen Department, she'd bumped into a couple of girlfriends and she'd told them how she really rated Dempsey's. This was praise indeed; the store had been given the royal seal of approval from the Shopping Queen.

Sharon and the girls had been very excited as

they made their arrangements for meeting up later. She had so much to tell them, she could barely find time to pause for a breath and had totally forgotten Danny. Later, when she had thought about his disappearance, she'd assumed he'd craftily, slipped away to his flat.

Shortly after Danny had fallen asleep, two young store men arrived pushing a high sided trolley with a wardrobe on it, and they'd been too engrossed in a conversation about a couple girls from the Beauty Department, to see Danny asleep on the armchair behind them.

They off-loaded the wardrobe next to one in front of him and then moved a sofa in front of that so Danny was totally obscured by furniture now. As they walked away, they made plans to leave work as soon as possible because they were going to a 'Mega Party' in Bath.

Danny was fast asleep, so he hadn't heard the message on the Tannoy system, as the girl announced that the store was closing in five minutes. But, even if he had been awake, he probably wouldn't have understood her because she had a broad Glaswegian accent and speech impediment and nearly all the other shoppers in the store were bemused by her message. They'd all asked each other afterwards-

'What did she say?'

Sharon phoned Danny again before going out to Wendy's house, but she hadn't been able to contact him and she assumed he must have switched off his mobile to get some undisturbed sleep.

THE FOURTH FLOOR, IN DEMPSEY'S. SATURDAY 2.35AM.

Danny woke up with a start because he'd sensed he was somewhere he shouldn't be. He was cold, it smelt strange and it was black as liquorice. He sat bolt upright and stared hard into the inert space in front of him, until slowly but surely, two big, dense black, rectangular shapes appeared in front of his eyes.

Shiiit! Where am I? I can't see anything. Have I gone blind, no don't be a twat. Am I dead? Where the hell am I? What's that smell, new furniture... Oh my God! I'm still in that store, what's its name? Dentskey's, no Dempsey's. His brain was working overtime as he struggled to work it out.

Bloody Hell! I must have fallen asleep. Great! What an idiot! Get yourself out of this one, you bloody fool. What a stupid jerk! He put his head in his hands and he combed his fingers through his hair as he tried to think of what to do next.

Where the hell is Sharon? She must have left me here, that's charming, it's her bloody fault, you wait' till I see her, I'll bloody kill her! Oh! Why didn't I pay more attention to this place when we arrived? I don't remember the layout, I can't even remember entering the store.

He was panicking now and then the answer came to him. 'Phone! Ha ha phooone!' He laughed and he smiled all smug, thinking he'd solved his problem and began to frisk himself quickly, looking for the bulge of his mobile phone in his trouser pockets, but he couldn't find it. So, he got down on his knees and began feeling on top of the armchair in front of him, and then checked down the sides frantically, just in case it had fallen out of his pocket, but he still couldn't find it. So he sat back down again thinking hard with his eyes closed, retracing his steps in his flat the morning before.

Then it hit him - he realised what he'd done. 'Agghhh!' he cried out, 'I left it on the bathroom shelf when I was shaving.' He began to deflate in the chair, not moving a muscle, he was totally defeated now.

But after a short while, he decided it was time for action. He stood up and began moving forward with his arms scything the air in front of him, like a blind man.

Thwack!

His fingers struck against the rough wood on the back of a wardrobe. 'Shit!' He cursed, more with the shock, than from the pain of it and stopped to hold onto his fingers for a while. After a few seconds of gentle massage the pain had subsided and he moved forward again. He couldn't see much, but he sensed he should squeeze his body through the narrow gap between the two wardrobes and although he was still disorientated by the blackness in the store, he continued until - *Thwump!*

Without warning, he'd hit the back of a sofa on the top of his thighs and somersaulted over it like a

Circus clown, ending up sat bolt upright on the floor with his legs wide apart. He was totally shocked by his experience.

'Idiot!' he shouted into the store, not caring if anybody heard him. He picked himself up again, he was so annoyed with the sofa he kicked it hard for dumping him down so abruptly and it made him feel a lot better. He looked around him, and he spied a dimly lit exit sign. He walked towards it, with his eyes still adjusting to the dark and by the time he'd arrived at the swing doors beneath the exit sign, he was able to see a lot clearer.

He pushed on through the doors and saw the lifts and the stairs in front of him. He decided he wouldn't risk a lift, just in case he got stuck in it and he took the stairs instead. The safety lights were doing a bad job in lighting them, so he hugged onto the cold, metal hand rail and slowly guided himself downwards, step by step until he'd reached the bottom of the stairs.

DEMPSEY'S BASEMENT. SATURDAY, 3AM.

He could see the double doors in front of him, and figured they would undoubtedly lead into a storeroom. He pushed them and was pleased to see they'd been left open by the store men, in their hurry to leave on Friday evening. He began to feel upbeat now because he was convinced that he would find an exit from there.

Good, not locked, that's the first bit of luck I've had! He thought as he was walking into the dark abyss and he began threading his way through the palettes, boxes and high sided trolleys left filled with goods, ready to replenish the shelves the following day. But, he made slow progress in the dark which was a major hindrance to him. How he would have loved to have switched on the lights, but he daren't; he mustn't be caught now.

What I'd give for a torch he thought as he moved on blindly through the obstacle course to find the exit in the dark. Using his animal instincts, he realised he had to tread carefully because he sensed some of the things around him were sharp and he felt them snag his clothes as he walked past.

Why didn't you just stay safe on the armchair upstairs and wait for the store to open? He asked himself.

Because, you didn't want to look like a complete and utter plonker when they found you. He answered.

Think how embarrassing it would be, having to explain what you are doing there in the middle of the night, for one. Sharon would kill you, for two. Your mates would never let you forget it, for three, then, there are your parents, four and the people at work, they might sack you! Five. No, they wouldn't, but, they would certainly think you are a cretin. And what if the papers got hold of the story, they'd have a field day, six.
He stopped and shut his eyes when he thought about the lengthening list. His thoughts were unbearable and the list was far too long to contemplate going back upstairs to wait for the store to open now.

Nothing for it, I've got to get out of this store and as soon as possible. I'm nearly out of here now anyway, I just need to find an exit and then..........

......what was that!

He'd heard a noise, like splintering wood.

Rats? – Oh no, don't let it be rats, I hate rats. There, there it is again, no, it's not rats; it sounds like... oh my God! It's human.

A beam of light appeared and Danny automatically veered off to his right and squatted down behind some large boxes. A beam swiped dangerously close to him and he closed his eyes ready for the end to come. The intruders were moving quietly, hardly making a sound as their beams cut the darkness around him, like laser swords.

Aliens! He thought for a moment.

Don't be daft you idiot, its thieves it's got to be thieves. Keep your head down and keep quiet, there's one of them now.

He couldn't really see them clearly, but instinctively began piecing together what he could see. *He's about six feet tall, skinny and wearing a hoodie, least I think it's a hoodie. Great! They'll catch him with a description like that, I don't think. Christ! This one's bigger than the first guy. No heroics now Danny. God, you're noisy when you breathe.*

The torch beam lit up things around him, so he ducked down even lower and closed his eyes again, holding onto his breath, but he couldn't do it for long because he felt faint. So, he risked opening his eyes again and tried breathing long, slow breaths instead. But, when he saw a third beam approaching him, he stopped breathing again.

He was very scared now, he could feel cold sweat forming on his forehead and he wiped it off slowly with his arm. Then he strained to see what the third burglar looked like in the half light.

About 5'9" with a baseball cap by the look of it. God, I wish I could see their faces. I wonder if Dempsey's will pay a reward. He was trying to turn his bad luck into some good fortune and then he saw a newspaper headline appear in his head;

'DANNY WALKER, LOCAL HERO, RISKS ALL, TO FOIL DEMPSEY'S BREAK-IN.'

…But hold on a minute, 'risks all,' that's the bit I don't like and where are the security guards? They're the ones paid

to be heroes. What the hell am I going to do? Stay where you are, don't panic, and pull yourself together. I wish I had a bag to blow into, I think I'm hyperventilating! God I need a pee.

Eventually, all three of them had past him by and he realised he'd been lucky in choosing his hiding place. Their beams moved away from him, towards the doors leading into the store, but before they left the basement they'd all converged and began talking quietly to each other. He couldn't hear what was being said, but, they were obviously working out what they were going to take and then they began emptying things out of crates not worrying about the mess.

He watched as they passed him again with empty crates and on returning they disappeared into the store. He waited patiently for what seemed like hours and then one by one they returned with designer clothes which they dumped into the crates, ready to take away later.

Suddenly he heard a noise. Someone else was at the door...

Who's that? Christ not another one!

STILL IN THE BASEMENT.
3.30AM.

A man in a uniform appeared in the doorway and with the bright light shining behind him, it made his shape soft around the edges.

It's a policeman? No, it's a security guard, I'm saved. Thank God! But, hold on a minute, what if they attack him? He's on his own and he's out numbered three to one. I should warn him. But hold on, they might jump on me? What if they've got knives or guns? I'd better stay where I am. Better safe than sorry, and hopefully he's called the police anyway. God I need that pee now!

Their torch beams turned on the guard and he recklessly stood his ground. He shone his torch into the eyes of the smallest burglar, who was nearest to him with his hands so fully laden with clothes, that only his eyes were visible.

'You prat! You scared me rigid,' he cursed, and the guard, began laughing at him like Muttley in the 'Wacky Races.'

'Get a move on Terry, you haven't got all night, I've got to switch the alarm back on soon and don't forget that perfume for your mother, or she'll kill me!'

Bloody Hell! The guard's in on it too and he's only the little one's old man. Danny's heart sank to rock bottom now.

The gang didn't hang around long, they all dispersed, back into the store again, looking for more things to steal and the guard didn't wait either, he'd turned back and walked the way he'd come. But, he'd been careless, he hadn't closed the door properly and a shard of light shone through it and landed on something red on the wall. Danny realised, it was one of those 'smash the glass' fire alarms, it had been too dark to see it earlier but now it was like a sign from God.

That's it, that's my way out of here, I'll smash the fire alarm and that will bring the fire brigade here. I'll be able to slip away in the confusion. Perfect; I might be caught if I hang around here anyway, so it's got to be worth a go.

The burglars had left the basement to look for more designer clothes on the floor above. So, Danny seized his opportunity and left the safety of his hiding place. He made his way towards the exit and on his way there, he picked up a small umbrella from a pile in an open box, it wasn't the best weapon, but it gave him the extra courage he needed to make his escape.

Moving quickly and with a new purpose now, he threaded his way through the boxes until he was poking his head out of the door, alert to every movement and every sound. He looked left and then right and saw the grey wire fence that was surrounding the yard in front of him and this was the only thing that was blocking his escape now. He could see the street lamp that had illuminated the alarm and it was picking out the

49

newly cut wire netting where the men had snipped the fence. The hole was directly in front of him, although it wasn't too obvious because the thieves had pulled the wire back into position after climbing through.

Conveniently, parked in road about ten yards from the hole, he saw an old white van and he figured it had to be theirs. *I can't see a driver, but, perhaps one of the others drove?* He didn't dare to wait any longer; he looked left and right a couple of times, and then smashed the glass on the fire alarm with the umbrella's hard plastic handle. It burst into life noisily and it made him jump. He hadn't appreciated that it would sound quite so loud.

All clear! Go! Go! Go!

He pushed the door away from him, and ran as fast as he could across the yard to the tear in the fence. He listened for the burglars behind him as he ran, but all he could hear was his own footsteps echoing in the yard. When he arrived at the fence he pulled the wire netting away from around the hole, but in his haste he lost his grip, and the wire whipped back across his face, scratching him and making him bleed.

He cursed out loud, it didn't matter how noisy he was now because the alarm was belting it out. He wiped the blood off his face on the sleeve of his jumper and quickly grabbed the wire again, only firmer this time and he pulled it back making the gash wide enough for him to squeeze through. He was free, running fast, skirting around the van at top speed, and then.......

...WOOAAAH!

There, in front of him, was a man mountain blocking his way and Danny couldn't believe the size of him. He stopped dead in his tracks as he'd realised it was the elusive driver and his fat face was crimson and awash with perspiration, due to the exertion of getting out of the van so quickly. He was grossly overweight and his whole body wobbled all over like a jelly and this explained why he'd taken so long getting out of the van. He caught a strong smell of sweat as the man moved closer to him.

'Come ere ya little sod,' he shouted lunging, but Danny was too nimble for him. He swerved away and swung the umbrella with a backhand, catching him on the bridge of his nose. The man cried out in pain as his nose flowered with a gush of blood and it shot out of him like a soda siphon. He staggered backwards and was only stopped from falling when his back hit the van.

'You little bastard!' He shouted out in a muffled voice gripping hold of his nose trying to stem the flow of blood. It had distracted him long enough, for Danny to make his escape and he kept on running without looking back. A brick wall appeared in front of him and he hurdled it, landing in the yard of the Tyre and Exhaust Company that was adjacent to the store. He felt like an athlete running in a relay race as he skirted around the building, still clutching the baton in left his hand, only, it wasn't a baton, it was the umbrella.

He chanced a little glance behind him now and luckily, there was nobody in sight. So, he slowed down and began walking fast as he tried to catch his breath. He'd felt the umbrella had hampered his running so he threw it down to the side of him, like Michael's assassin's gun, in the first 'Godfather' film.

In the background, he could hear the gang now, shouting and cursing him and boy they were mad!

He started running again and soon he reached the front of the tyre company. He crossed over the road and jumped another low wall that was surrounding a car park in front of a red brick office building. He slid down it until he was sitting on the other side and he could feel the cold dampness of the bricks against his back where his shirt and jumper had rucked-up.

His chest was hurting as he refilled his aching lungs. But he soon stopped doing it, when he heard the sound of running feet in the road behind him.

'Here they come!' Danny needed to see what they were up to, so he glanced to the left and noticed a thin gap under some fence panels sat on top of the wall. They'd been erected there, to hide the dustbins from the public's gaze. Keeping low, he crawled on his hands and knees to peer through the gap under the fence. The lanky burglar was with the security guard in the middle of the road, and they'd stopped running now to catch their breath. Both of them were puffing and

wheezing and the guard was bent double resting his hands on his knees. They were listening out for him, and trying to see a sign of where he might be hiding.

'He's run to ground Pete,' the guard shouted out to the burglar in between gasps of breath.

'Yeah! But, we can't hang around here any longer; the fire brigade will be here soon.'

They could hear the sirens getting closer by the second and they realised they were running out of time.

'We'll have to scarper, you'd better go back to the store to get rid of them,' spat the lanky crook, and as an after thought he yelled 'You'd better keep your mouth shut kid, or you're a dead man!'

Danny thought his heart had stopped beating when he heard this threat and he was mightily relieved, when he saw the men turn and start running back towards the store. His eyes closed and he said a little 'thank you' to God for letting him escape.

He stayed behind the wall for about ten minutes afterwards, watching for them, even though they were long gone. He was being extra cautious after the death threat and eventually he found the courage to stand up again. He walked back towards the front of the store like a Neanderthal, stooping low, keeping to the shadows, alert, and ready to run.

IN FRONT OF THE STORE.
FRIDAY 4AM.

Three fire engines and a police car were blocking the road in front of Dempsey's, their lights were flashing and their headlights were trained on the entrance. The firemen were all busy, milling around the building as they searched for signs of the fire. Danny was crouched behind a car, looking at the policemen.

One of them had thin black moustache and an olive complexion and Danny figured he was probably Italian. The other one was thick set, with short fair hair and he was sat in the passenger side of the police car with its door wide open and he had his back turned to him. He was talking into the car radio, so Danny waited patiently for him to finish and then approached him.

As he got closer, he could see the security guard with the Italian officer on the other side of the car and they were walking towards the front of the store. The guard was still trying to convince him that it was all a false alarm, however, the policeman tried the revolving doors a few times anyway to check if doors were locked.

When Danny arrived at the car he said.

'Can I have a word with you officer?' And he made the fair-haired policeman jump because he hadn't seen him coming out of the dark. He stared at the scratch on Danny's face suspiciously.

'Is it important sir? As you can see, I'm a bit busy at the moment,' he replied, in an attempt to get rid of him.

'Yes, it is.' Danny was annoyed with him, and refused to be deterred.

'There was an attempted break- in at Dempsey's tonight and I was a witness to it. If you follow me, I'll show you where the gang cut through the fence to get in, and that security guard over there was party to it. He's trying to steer you and your colleague away from the evidence.' Danny nodded towards the guard as he said this, but, he was very careful not to let him hear.

The policeman climbed out of his car, laboriously and he was wondering if he was crazy to be listening to this young man who'd been out wandering the streets at such a late hour. But, he followed him patiently and when they'd arrived at the hole in the fence, Danny said-

'They got in here.' And he pointed towards the tear in the wire. The policeman began inspecting it and immediately he noticed something red...

'Blood!' He said and then looked at the scratch on Danny's face again. Danny said nothing to him, not wishing to incriminate himself.

The policeman helped Danny climb through the wire netting and he followed on after him, carefully so as not to touch the blood as he squeezed through the hole. They walked through the yard to the side door and Danny was worried as it appeared to be closed.

But then he was relieved, when he saw there were still signs of the door having been forced. The crooks had been very brutal with the door frame because they hadn't wanted it to appear like an inside job and now the door wouldn't shut properly.

The policeman eased the door open with with a gloved hand, careful not to smudge any fingerprints and Danny followed him into the store. The officer's torch shone around the store room and the beam rested on the crates they'd prepared to take with them.

'They left those crates behind and there's the alarm I smashed to bring you heeeer…..' He didn't quite finish what he was saying because he'd realised, he'd said too much and the fair-haired policeman was quick to catch on.

'So you were in the store then?'

'Well, yes, but…' Danny knew it was too late to say anything different now, but then, why should he?

Bloody hell! Things could get awkward for me now, he thought to himself.

'I'll explain all that to you afterwards officer, just let me tell you what I know about the robbery first. Surely you need to make a call to someone - you know, to catch them? He said sarcastically. He didn't wait for the policeman's response and he began recounting all he could about the crooks. Danny was pleased by what he'd remembered, considering how tired he was.

'They had a dirty white, L. reg. van, with rust around the wheel arches.

The near side back bumper was all bashed- in and the aerial was snapped off with a coat hanger in its place. There were four men in the gang, the driver was a big, red-faced man with black curly hair and he must have weighed about twenty stones, or more.'

Danny had retained good detail about the driver and particularly the lanky burglar who he'd especially wanted caught, after he'd threatened to kill him. The policeman had found it hard to keep up with Danny as he'd regurgitated all the facts to him. He'd scribbled down spider crawl notes in his little black book until Danny had finished his debrief by saying…

'So let me assure you officer, I had nothing to do with this robbery, I simply fell asleep in the 'store and became a witness to it.'

The policeman stopped him there and said,

'What's your name?' Danny was frustrated by this, as he'd been asked such a trivial question after the quality information he'd been giving him, and he sighed as he answered.

'Daniel Walker. Look officer, I will co-operate with you in every way I can – but please think, if I had been in on it, I would hardly have come looking for you, now would I? I would have gone home to get some sleep, which I'm in desperate need of. I honestly don't know how I'm still able to talk to you, I'm so tired and I have a friend's wedding to go to tomorrow; so can we concentrate on catching the crooks.' Danny realised he probably shouldn't have been so rude, but he was so tired and desperate to go home.

The policeman ignored his comment and he began to radio over the description of the van to his colleagues so they could look out for it. He'd listened very carefully to Danny when he'd been recounting the details to him, but now he'd turned his back on him and was virtually ignoring him. As he was talking, he playfully kicked around some pieces of wood that had been dislodged from the door frame and after the call; he flicked his notebook back open again and started talking at the point where they had finished off.

'I know this may sound strange to you Mr. Walker, but you've admitted being inside the store at three o'clock this morning, okay, as you say, having fallen asleep, but, it's not a normal thing for people to do you know. So, I'm not saying I don't believe you, but it's hard to accept your story on face value. You'd be amazed at the tales I hear in the course of a day's work and believe it or not, not everyone tells me the truth.'

'Okay, I take your point,' Danny said, he was much too tired to argue with him.

'All right, let's go back to the car then shall we, I've just got to get a little bit more information from you.' The policeman would not be distracted, and on the way back to the car they bumped into his colleague and the security guard, who was still with him.

'Alright Ken? The security guard here thinks it was probably a fault on the alarm system… who's that with you?' His colleague enquired when he saw Danny.

God, what's going to happen now? Danny wondered and he looked at the guard who was staring viciously at him. Tiny beads of sweat had begun dribbling down his temples and Danny sensed that he would like to do something nasty to him to shut him up. So, he repositioned himself behind the big fair-haired policeman, who replied 'This gentleman here thinks not. He says, he set off the alarm.'

And, before he could say any more, the guard broke in on their conversation,

'Well done officer, you've caught the little runt, it's amazing what they'll do these days, I'm pretty sure that this is the guy I let off earlier. I caught him shop lifting with his gang and the lies he came out with then, you've got to watch him; he's got a very vivid imagination. I gave him the benefit of the doubt earlier on, but I regret it now. This is the way they repay you when you let 'em off. I don't know, it always comes back to haunt you.' He shook his head and his eyes rose to the heavens, dramatically.

The neck on this guy, it's unbelievable, how he could he work out his story so quickly and he lies so convincingly. He's so good at it, I almost believe him myself. Danny was worried now that the police might believe the guard's story and not his. Everything seemed to be stacking up against him, but, he couldn't let the man's lies go without trying to give his side of the story.

'That's a bloody lie! Don't listen to him officers.

I'm telling you, he was in on the robbery and now he's trying to put the blame on me.' He blurted out desperately, but it sounded so lame after the guard's polished performance.

'Robbery? What robbery? You see what I mean lads?' The guard was shaking his head in feigned disbelief and the policemen looked at each other, not knowing who to believe. The guard winked at Danny, which incensed him even more.

This guy is better at winding up people, than my mate Steve. He thought.

'Don't believe him officers, he's bloody lying I tell you, for God's sake, you have to believe me,' he protested, in desperation.

'Oh he's good, he's very good, he's a real pro, you see what I mean about his lies chaps and has he explained what he was doing here at this time of the night? I can't wait for this; this should be a good un.' He said smirking.

'He says he fell asleep in the store,' the fair-haired officer answered naively.

'Paah! Unbelievable,' said the guard laughing. 'I've heard it all now. I don't know, in all my years, couldn't you think of anything better than that kid? It's obvious what's happened here lads, he's tried to break into the store with his young punk friends and one of them has been cack-handed and broke the alarm. He's dreamt up this farcical story about falling asleep in the store, to allow them to get away.

60

That really does take the biscuit that does, what a liar!'

'Well, all I know is that there has been an attempt by someone's gang, to rob the store tonight. The fence has been cut by the side of the store in Gravel Street and the side door has been forced. I've also noticed a lot of blood on the road, on the pavement and some on the fence. So, we need to get to the bottom of that too.' The fair-haired officer replied unwaveringly.

A senior fire officer walked up to them now and broke-in on their conversation, he'd been listening, patiently, waiting for his chance to talk to the police officers.

'We're off now lads, it all looks okay here, well no fire anyway. I'll submit my report, if you'll do the rest.'

'Okay, will do,' the policemen said together, as if they'd practiced it and then the fair-haired officer said,

'Right! We'd better get the S.O.C. boys in here, for a bit of finger printing.'

He turned towards the guard again and said-

'Mr. Woods isn't it?' The guard nodded in reply.

'Officer Rossi here, will want to take a few more details from you, like how we can get hold of you, when your shift ends etc. Oh! And check the CCTV Tony.

The fair-haired policeman turned his attention back to Danny now, who was yawning like a black hole.

'And I'll have another little talk with this chap here; if he can stay awake long enough that is,' he said smirking as he'd enjoyed his little joke which had been cracked at Danny's expense. Danny wasn't amused, he was worried and he wished he hadn't annoyed the officer now.

'I'll take the car then Tony, while you go and talk with Mr. Woods in his office.' His colleague nodded at him and then walked away with the guard.

'If you'll come with me then Mr. Walker, it'll be warmer inside the car, as I think you'll agree, it's getting a bit 'parky' out ere.'

Danny was ushered into the back of the police car and the policeman climbed into the front. He introduced himself properly now, apparently his name was Murphy.

'Now, let's start from the beginning shall we,' he said to Danny as he found a new page in his notebook and Danny groaned.

'Look, officer, I've got to get some sleep, I'm going to a wedding tomorrow.' And as soon as he'd said it, he'd wished he hadn't.

'I promise I won't keep you any longer than I have to Mr. Walker and I'm sure you would prefer to talk here rather than us having to go back to the station. It will be much quicker sir and we *are* trying to catch the thieves aren't we?' He said sarcastically, enjoying his little revenge.

'And, of course we will try to get you to your wedding.'

Danny nodded his head in approval as he'd been put in his place, good and proper.

'Right, Danny, you don't mind me calling you Danny do you?'

Danny shook his head.

'Let's start with the blood in the road, on the pavement and on the fence? I notice you've got a nasty scratch on your face and blood on your sleeve. How did that get there?'

Danny closed his eyes again and was thinking.

How on earth did I get myself into this mess?

IN THE BACK OF THE POLICE CAR. SATURDAY, 6AM.

Danny was still in the back of the police car two hours later, having painfully recounted his story to PC Murphy again.

He'd explained how he had been on the three stag nights and how he'd not slept in the days to recover from them. This, he hoped would explain why he had fallen asleep in the store. The police officer was keen to know how the blood got on the fence and on the road. Danny described how he had scratched his face on the wire netting and how he'd used the umbrella, to hit the fat man to escape from his grasp.

At one point PC Murphy had made small talk and asked what they had done to the groom. Danny told him what he could remember and PC Murphy worked-out, that Phil and Pete were the lads he had found tied naked to the lamp post outside the Police station early on friday morning. He informed Danny that he had spoken with Steve Harris about them, as he was the only one sober enough to talk!

Steve had asked PC Murphy to lock Phil and Pete up in a cell over night, for a laugh and the officer told him that he had because of the sign hung around Phil's neck. Danny quickly moved him off the subject as he was the one who had painted the sign, and he was in enough trouble as it was.

'Isn't it a small world though, me knowing Steve and all' PC Murphy said smiling at him.

'Oh so you know Steve?' Danny exclaimed, shocked by this sudden revelation.

Apparently Steve had taken his sister out a couple of times, and he had meet PC Murphy when he had picked her up.

PC Murphy had made copious notes as he listened to Danny's sleepy tale. It had taken him much longer than expected because the policeman had interupted him several times to claify points and answer calls on his radio in between. The Scene of Crime Officers arrival hadn't helped - they'd stopped him mid-story to take his fingerprints.

It dawned on Danny that the only prints they would find would be his, as the crooks had all worn gloves. This meant that the only evidence they would find would point to him.

He could see a new newspaper headline in his head now; it was on the front page of the Evening Post

'WALKER WALKS THE WALK, FOR SUPERSTORE RAID!'

He could see a picture of himself in his minds eye, he was leaving the court with his hands cuffed and his mother and Sharon were crying uncontrollably.

This just gets worse, they're going to lock me up and throw away the key!

STILL IN THE POLICE CAR.
SATURDAY, 9AM.

Danny felt his shoulder being shaken and he woke with a start.

'It's time for bed now Danny,' the voice said and Danny recognised it, as belonging to PC Murphy.

Sleepily, he looked around to see where he was.

'As you can see, we've brought you home as it was on our way back to the station and we figured you wouldn't mind sleeping in the back of the car. You know, you really ought to get to bed earlier or you don't know where you'll end up sleeping next,' he quipped cruelly.

'By the way, we've got some good news for you, we've caught the gang, they decided not to waste the night and they had a go at a warehouse on the other side of town. One of the lads recognised their van from your description. It was parked in a side street next to a warehouse they were robbing and they caught them as they'd tried to leave. So, it's been a good night, we've cleared up two robberies.

I was wondering if you wouldn't mind coming down to the station on Monday morning to see if you can pick the men out in a line-up.'

Danny thought about it. He didn't really want to, but after a short pause, he replied 'Yeah okay, why not.'

He was so relieved that they had caught them, that he'd agreed to do it.

'What about the guard at the store?' Danny enquired.

'Oh yes, he was quite believable wasn't he. I must say, he had me believing him at one point, but, we checked the CCTV footage and found some nice shots of you and your girlfriend shopping and then some more of you, doing your Sleeping Beauty act. There was no sign of you being with a gang of shoplifters where he said he'd spoken to you, so I guess you're in the clear.'

However! We haven't got anything on the guard yet, other than he's a compulsive liar. He has an old record for a small indiscretion, but it was quite some time ago, so, we think your evidence could help us here. You say you heard him talking to his son in the store?'

Danny nodded.

'Well, we'll talk about that on Monday. Thanks for your help; you know we couldn't have caught them without you. It's a pity more people aren't as helpful. Mind you, it was a bit of luck you being there in the first place, but don't do it again, hey? You know you really could have got yourself into a lot of trouble.'

Danny nodded as he thought how lucky he'd been.

'Well, we'll see you on Monday then. We'll let you sleep in a bit; is 10am alright, not too early for you?'

He said grinning, thinking he was very funny and his colleague grinned too.

Danny just shook his head as he climbed out of the police car and embraced the fresh morning air.

'By the way, send my regards to Steve.' PC Murphy shouted out to him from the open car window.

'Okay!' Danny replied nervously. But, he was really thinking, *not bloody likely mate!, he's the last guy I'm going to tell about this*! He hoped that this whole embarrassing incident, this nasty little glitch in his normally, tidy life, would evaporate and disappear forever.

Danny watched as the car, grew smaller and smaller and then finally disappeared. He started to climb the stairs to his front door wearily, as if it was the North face of the Eager and with every step he took, he thought.

I must get some sleep.

DANNY'S FLAT SATURDAY. 9.25AM.

Danny let himself into his flat and walked straight- legged like a zombie to his bed. He prised off his trainers using his toes and kicked them off in front of him. Then he allowed himself to fall flat on his face like felled tree and with a groan of ecstasy 'Aaaahhhh!' And as soon as his face had hit the pillow, he was asleep.

But, half an hour later, he was woken again by his door buzzer; it reminded him of 'Groundhog Day.'

He was still lying face down on top of his bed with his arm flopped over the side and his hand was resting on one of his trainers on the floor. So, he picked it up and threw it backwards as hard as he could with a grunt. He had to stop the annoying buzzing sound at all cost, but his throw lacked skill and it missed the door completely. The trainer knocked off some books from a shelf instead and eventually it bounced to rest on the floor. He slid off his bed and walked on his hands and knees towards his front door because he had to stop the buzzing.

'Who's there?' His voice croaked as he shouted out at the bottom of the door. His eyes were clenched shut and his head had flopped down as if he was a grazing horse.

'Don't be bloody stupid Danny, hurry up and let me in. We've got to get to the pub and have a drink with the others.'

'Go away.' He groaned at her rudely.

'Let me in Danny Walker, this minute or by God I'll make you suffer. You didn't go out again last night did you?' Sharon was mad with him now.

He climbed up the door frame, like a lizard until he'd found the door catch and it clicked open. As soon as Sharon realised it had, she burst in, pushing past him like she was leading an SAS raid and she wasn't taking any prisoners this morning.

'What the hell's wrong with you? Leaving me out there like that; you'd better not spoil today.

'Are you ill or something?' And what's that scratch on your face?' Her questions rattled out like bullets from a gattling gun. 'Have you been fighting?'

'No I haven't. It's a long story, I've only had a couple of hour's sleep, in fact I've only just got in.'

'What! What on earth have doing now?'

But, before he could tell her, she'd looked at her wrist watch and said,

'Actually, don't bother, if we're going to make the pub, your story will have to wait.'

She was blinkered by the wedding, it was more important to her than anything he could tell her today.

'Have a shower and a shave, while I go and get some fags at the newsagent's and wear your new suit with your blue tie, you know, the one I bought you.'

'Yes dear,' he said sarcastically, he didn't have the energy to argue with her today and then he turned around and began peeling off his clothes, dropping them on the floor as he plodded towards the shower.

THE NEWSAGENT.
10.30AM SATURDAY.

Sharon had turned on her heels and was gone from his flat in an instant, although she'd almost turned back because she had regretted not finding out what had happened to him. Then it dawned on her; he hadn't complimented her on the way she looked. She made a mental note to give him a hard time for that later.

She'd set off for the newsagent's at a quick lick, dressed in her new mauve wedding outfit with a matching wide brimmed hat and the wind had tried to rip it off her head several times as she walked up the road. So she'd held on to it all the way to the shop. She felt good in her new clothes as they made her feel like a Hollywood film actress bound for the Oscars. Dave the news agent had laid on his compliments thick when she'd arrived at the shop, and he'd commented on how sexy she looked in her new clothes. As always he flirted with her outrageously and she'd enjoyed it as he'd made her feel special. She loved dressing up and she couldn't wait to see what the other girls would be wearing at the Wedding

'That's the beauty of weddings you see Dave, you have to buy something special and it doesn't really matter how much it costs because you've got to look your best. I'd better buy extra cigarettes today, to get me through the celebrations as it's going to be a long day *and* night.'

72

'I bet,' said Dave, with a 'Carry on film' innuendo and a lusty grin.

'Oh give over,' she replied in the Barbara Windsor role.

After a little more small talk, she bought forty cigarettes then said her goodbyes. She walked back down the road in a good mood and her heels were clacking like castanets. As she got closer to Danny's flat she spied him sitting on the low partition wall at the front of his house, waiting for her like a faithful labrador. His hair was still wet and the water was dribbling down the back of his neck after his shower. He'd closed is eyes again and his tie was askew. The first thing she did on arriving was to yank it around hard and then tighten it for him. This woke him up abruptly.

'Wake up dozy! Honestly, it's like going out with a bloody kid, I reckon you've got sleeping sickness or something, I swear I've never known anyone like you for sleeping.' She pulled him up.

'Come on; let's get you to the car.' She led him to it by his tie and opened the door for him. He fell onto the passenger seat and closed his eyes again. She got in on the driver's side and before he could settle, she calmly asked.

'Okay then, tell me what happened.'

SHARON'S CAR.
11.45 AM SATURDAY.

He'd only just finished giving her his abridged version of the events that had happened after she'd left him in the store on Friday evening, when they arrived in the pub car park. She had been trying to keep up with his story, whilst concentrating on her driving and she'd interrupted his flow about fifty times, in trying to clarify the finer points. And he'd said.

'For God's sake woman, if you shut up I will tell you,' in as many times in his reply to her. He'd tried to blame her for leaving him asleep in the store, but she wasn't having it.

'Oh no you don't, it was your stupid fault, don't try blaming me.'(Score 1-0) Game over, no arguments, not this time.

They pulled into an empty space and as they were unbuckling their seat belts, she said to him.

'Well, I just don't know what to say to you Danny, except, you're a bloody idiot!' And she began laughing at him in an uncontrollable fit of giggles and when she'd thought she'd finished, she began to mop up her mascara because her tears had made it run down her cheeks. But then, she began laughing again, when she thought about him waking up in the store in the middle of the night.

'It's not funny Shaz,' he bleated in a little boy's voice.

'Isn't it,' she said and then began laughing again.

'I could have been beaten to death!'

'Oh stop it Danny, I'm going to wet myself', she said trying to hold back her giggles.

'I could. I could have died!'

Her laugh was so infectious, and he was so embarrassed, he couldn't help but laugh with her now.

After a few more minutes, she began tidying her make-up again and he started to plead with her.

'Please don't tell them in there Shaz, I'm begging you. They'll crucify me.' He'd motioned with his head towards their friends, who he expected would be in the Queens Head.

'We'll see. I can't promise though,' she said, snapping her make-up case closed. After they got out of the car, she made one more check of her face in a side mirror and they walked towards the entrance of the pub.

THE QUEENS HEAD PUB.
11.50AM SATURDAY.

They pushed the swing doors and entered the Lounge. All their friends were in front of them, dressed in their finery around the bar and they turned around to watch them enter. It was like an ambush and the next few moments seemed to pass in slow motion, like in the closing scene in 'Butch Cassidy and the Sundance Kid.' And then Steve Harris's face came into the frame and he shouted out in a loud voice.

'Look out, here comes 'Rip Van Winkle!' All their friends cheered and pointed at poor Danny and some of them pretended to fall asleep, clasping their hands to the side of their faces, like they were pillows.

Danny, turned bright red with embarrassment and then he realised they all knew what had happened to him and he said grinning at them -

'Okay you sods, the jokes over now. How the hell did you find out about it?'

Steve moved forward and introduced a pretty, fair-haired girl to him who was stood by his side.

'You haven't met my new girlfriend have you Dan?

'This is Kate... Kate Murphy... you know...PC Murphy's sister!'

EPILOGUE

Pete looked good in his top hat and tails, in fact he looked a proper toff, but it didn't suit Phil as he'd never looked smart out of casual clothes. The large red welt on his forehead (after head butting the urinal on his stag night) and a cut from shaving made him look like he had been beaten up. He was a bag of nerves, and wished he'd not drunk so much in the Queens Head now because he was desperate to go to the toilet. However, he'd not muddled any of his words in the wedding service and it all went to plan. The only error made was by the vicar, who'd mistakenly called him 'Paul' and Wendy 'Sue'. After they'd corrected him, he'd said awkwardly,

'I'm sorry, they were the couple I married this morning,' and everybody laughed.

Wendy was more embarrassed when Phil rushed-off to the toilet after the 'kissing the bride.' In his haste he'd left the door open and the congregation were treated to the sounds of his steady flow of water and his sighs of relief because the church organ hadn't been able to drown them out.

Numerous photographs were taken in the churchyard afterwards, and then the couple made their way to the reception hotel in a pony and trap.

After the wedding meal, came the speeches. Phil kept his short, restricting it to thanking everyone, and Pete's best man's speech was well received too as he was good at telling jokes and he'd bolstered it with tales from the stag night celebrations.

He finished his speech off saying -

' …and of course we'd like to thank Avon and Somerset police, for releasing Danny our sleepy usher, me, and of course Phil, so that we were all able to attend this wonderful wedding with you here today.'

All the guests had appreciated his joke, all but Danny, who'd squirmed with embarrassment and Phil who'd just smiled and avoided Wendy's glare because she'd just found out about his night in the cells. Sharon caught the bouquet after Wendy threw it over her shoulder; she'd wrestled another girl for it and won. She'd never liked her and now she was in her element. You would have thought it was her wedding night.

Danny, Steve and a select party of the 'Spurs,' had come well prepared with toilet rolls, lipstick, cans and condoms and they'd sneaked off into the car park to decorate their car. Phil had cursed them when he'd seen what they'd done to it, but he'd guessed it would happen as it was a tradition now. Wendy was not impressed with the state of the car as he pulled up in the front of the hotel, but their friends and relations had all cheered. They'd shouted their goodbyes as the happy couple turned out of the hotel grounds and after they had departed, Sharon began looking for Danny because she hadn't seen him waving goodbye. She'd asked everyone she'd bumped into if they'd seen him, but they hadn't. He'd disappeared again!

After exhausting her search inside, she went into the garden to have a cigarette and her eyes were drawn to the white mess in the middle of the hotel lawn.

The swinging garden seat was festooned in toilet roll, cans and confetti. She'd found him. Danny was on it fast asleep and he'd been decorated too!

THE END

ACKNOWLEDGEMENTS

Many thanks to Lucy Williams, Lucy Shepherd, David Mair and David Price for agreeing to read my book and for their constructive feedback. And a real big, big thanks to Jer Stephens who encouraged me to write it in the first place.

ELWORTHY
Office Supplies

Commercial Stationers & Office Equipment Specialists

Tel: 0117 9737252
Fax: 0117 9736187

Email: sales@elworthy.co.uk
Web: www.elworthy.co.uk

Elworthy Office Supplies
185 Redland Road, Redland, Bristol, BS6 6XP

Ambience Landscapes ltd

0117 971 1742

www.ambiencelandscapes.co.uk

Broomhill Nurseries, Ironmould Lane,
Brislington, Bristol, BS4 5RS